A DAY IN THE LIFE OF A COMMUNITY SERVICE VEHICLE

A DAY IN THE LIFE OF A GARBAGE TRUCK

by Nicole A. Mansfield

PEBBLE
a capstone imprint

Published by Pebble, an imprint of Capstone
1710 Roe Crest Drive, North Mankato, Minnesota 56003
capstonepub.com

Copyright © 2025 by Capstone. All rights reserved. No part of this publication may be reproduced in whole or in part, or stored in a retrieval system, or transmitted in any form or by any means, electronic, mechanical, photocopying, recording, or otherwise, without written permission of the publisher.

Library of Congress Cataloging-in-Publication Data is available on the Library of Congress website.
ISBN: 9780756586980 (hardcover)
ISBN: 9780756586935 (paperback)
ISBN: 9780756586942 (ebook PDF)

Summary: Rumble! A large garbage truck turns the corner. It stops along the street curb. The truck's metal arm lifts a garbage can. The trash dumps into the truck's hopper. The truck gets fuller. Later, the driver dumps the garbage at the landfill. Learn what garbage trucks do day in and day out!

Editorial Credits
Editor: Carrie Sheely; Designer: Elyse White; Media Researcher: Jo Miller; Production Specialist: Tori Abraham

Image Credits
Alamy: ZUMA Press Inc, 8; AP Images: Armando Franca, 19; Getty Images: Alistair McLellan, 6, Benjamin44, 9, DoganKutukcu, 15, Don Mason, 5, 21, Scott Olson, 16; Houston Chronicle/Hearst Newspapers via Getty Images, 18; Shutterstock: Another77, cover (front and back), Fotana, 20 (pens), hedgehog94, 13, MikeDotta, 14, New Africa, 20 (paper), Real Window Creative, 12, Rob Crandall, 7, Virrage Images, 11, 17

Any additional websites and resources referenced in this book are not maintained, authorized, or sponsored by Capstone. All product and company names are trademarks™ or registered® trademarks of their respective holders.

Printed and bound in China. 6097

TABLE OF CONTENTS

Hard Work 4

An Early Start.. 6

Collection Time 8

Unloading 12

The Day's End 16

    Garbage Truck Art 20

    Glossary 22

    Read More 23

    Internet Sites 23

    Index 24

    About the Author 24

Words in **bold** are in the glossary.

HARD WORK

Vroom! A huge truck rumbles. People hear its loud engine. It is on its way to collect trash.

Garbage trucks are service vehicles. They collect trash in our **communities**. **Waste** collectors are workers who use garbage trucks.

AN EARLY START

Garbage trucks leave the waste station early in the morning. There are few cars on the road. The trucks are on their way to homes. A garbage truck can collect trash from more than 1,000 homes a day!

Some trucks pick up **recyclable** materials too. These can include glass and plastic bottles. They include cardboard too. The materials might go in a different part of the truck than trash.

COLLECTION TIME

People leave their trash cans along the street. A side-loader truck has an **automated** metal arm. The arm lifts up the garbage cans. The driver uses a joystick to move the arm.

joystick

The trash dumps into the truck's **hopper**.
Then a **compactor** squeezes the trash.
Squash! Now there is room for more!

Most waste collectors do their jobs from the **cabin**. They use controllers to move the truck's parts. They only get out to solve a problem.

Drivers look at camera screens. They can see the truck parts move. The truck's mirrors show if people or animals are too close to the truck.

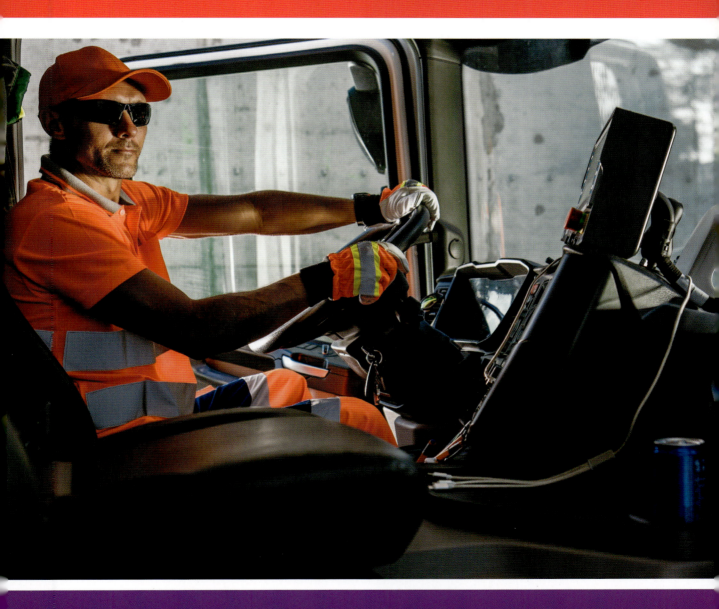

UNLOADING

Now, the truck is full of trash. Its next stop is the landfill. A landfill is where the truck dumps its trash. There is a traffic jam on the way! The truck's **navigation system** shows maps and directions. The driver stays away from the traffic jam.

Navigation system

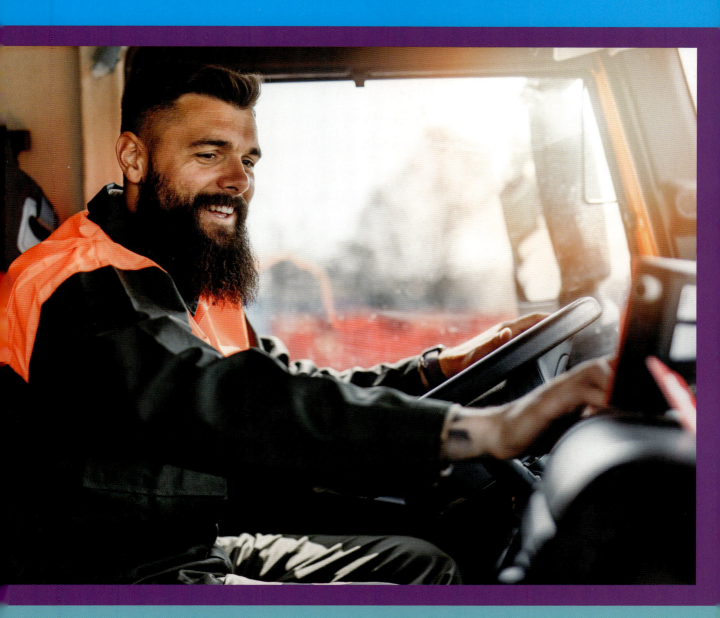

At the landfill, the garbage truck backs up close to the dumping area. The driver uses a button to open the tailgate. The **discharge plates** push the trash out. Whoosh!

14

Recyclable materials go to a recycling center. The materials are sorted there.

Recycling center

THE DAY'S END

It's late afternoon when the garbage truck returns to the station. The truck is washed with a sprayer. This helps keep the truck from smelling bad.

Hose for natural gas refueling

The garbage truck parks. The trucks are refilled with fuel. Some trucks use **diesel fuel**. Other trucks run on **natural gas**. Natural gas burns cleaner than diesel fuel.

The garbage trucks are done for the night. They will be busy at work again tomorrow!

GARBAGE TRUCK ART

You learned a lot about what garbage trucks do all day. Now, let's make a drawing showing all of their parts.

What You Need:

- the pictures in this book
- white paper or poster board
- markers

What You Do:

1. Start at the beginning of this book. Look at all of the pictures of garbage trucks.

2. Pick your favorite one.

3. On the paper or poster board, use markers to do your best drawing.

4. Label the hopper, cabin, tires, and arm on your picture.

5. Show and tell family or friends about your garbage truck art.

GLOSSARY

automate (AW-toe-mayt)—to do a job using a machine

cabin (KA-buhn)—the part of a truck where waste collectors sit

community (kuh-MYOO-nuh-tee)—a group of people who live in the same area

compactor (kum-PAKT-or)—a part that squeezes garbage in a truck's hopper

diesel fuel (DEE-zuhl FYOOL)—a heavy oil that burns to make power

discharge plate (dis-CHARJ PLAYT)—a big metal plate that pushes trash out of a garbage truck

natural gas (NACH-ur-uhl GAS)—a gas made in the earth that can be burned

navigation system (NAV-uh-gay-shuhn SISS-tuhm)—a system that shows the best route to take

recyclable (ree-SY-kuhl-ah-buhl)—able to be used again

waste (WAYST)—trash

READ MORE

Dickmann, Nancy. *Garbage Trucks*. North Mankato, MN: Capstone, 2021.

Kaiser, Brianna. *All about Garbage Collectors*. Minneapolis: Lerner, 2022.

McDonald, Amy. *Garbage Trucks*. Minneapolis: Bellwether Media, 2021.

INTERNET SITES

Ducksters: The Environment: Recycling
ducksters.com/science/environment/recycling_for_kids.php

National Geographic: Landfills
education.nationalgeographic.org/resource/landfills

PBS: Riding Inside the Cab at the Garbage Truck Road-eo
pbs.org/video/riding-inside-the-cab-at-the-garbage-truck-road-eo-crvecq

INDEX

cabins, 10
camera screens, 10
compactors, 9
diesel fuel, 18
hoppers, 9
landfills, 12, 14

natural gas, 18
navigation systems, 12
recyclable materials, 7, 15
side-loader trucks, 8
stations, 6, 16

ABOUT THE AUTHOR

Nicole Mansfield is a mother of three, a wife, and educator. She enjoys singing and leading church worship music every chance that she gets! She is passionate about eating well and exercising. Nicole lives in the great state of Texas with her military family.